Note to parents, carers and teachers

Read it yourself is a series of modern stories, favourite characters and traditional tales written in a simple way for children who are learning to read. The books can be read independently or as part of a guided reading session.

Each book is carefully structured to include many high-frequency words vital for first reading. The sentences on each page are supported closely by pictures to help with understanding, and to offer lively details to talk about.

The books are graded into four levels that progressively introduce wider vocabulary and longer stories as a reader's ability and confidence grows.

Ideas for use

• Begin by looking through the book and talking about the pictures. Has your child heard this story before?

• Help your child with any words he does not know, either by helping him to sound them out or supplying them yourself.

• Developing readers can be concentrating so hard on the words that they sometimes don't fully grasp the meaning of what they're reading. Answering the puzzle questions on pages 30 and 31 will help with understanding.

For more information and advice on Read it yourself and book banding, visit **www.ladybird.com/readityourself**

Book
Band
7

Level 2 is ideal for children who have received some reading instruction and can read short, simple sentences with help.

Special features:

Frequent repetition of main story words and phrases

Short, simple sentences

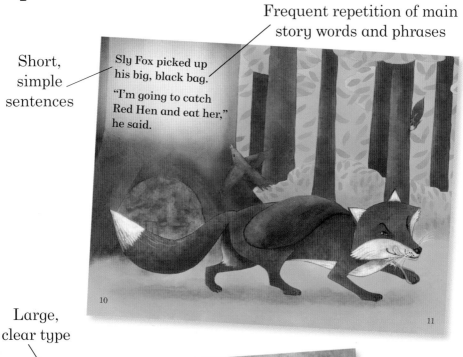

Sly Fox picked up his big, black bag.

"I'm going to catch Red Hen and eat her," he said.

10

11

Large, clear type

Careful match between story and pictures

"I will catch you," said Sly Fox, and he ran round and round and round.

16

17

Educational Consultant: Geraldine Taylor
Book Banding Consultant: Kate Ruttle

A catalogue record for this book is available from the British Library

Published by Ladybird Books Ltd
80 Strand, London, WC2R 0RL
A Penguin Company

004

ISBN: 978-0-72327-280-9

Printed in China

Sly Fox
and Red Hen

Illustrated by Diana Mayo

Red Hen lived in a
little house in a tree.

Sly Fox lived in the wood.
And he was hungry.

Sly Fox picked up his big, black bag.

"I'm going to catch Red Hen and eat her," he said.

Sly Fox hid in Red Hen's little house.

"I'm the fox, I'm the fox, I'm really sly. You can't beat me, however you try!" said Sly Fox.

Red Hen saw Sly Fox and jumped up out of his way.

"You're the fox, you're the fox, you're really sly. But you won't catch me, however you try!" said Red Hen.

"I will catch you," said Sly Fox, and he ran round and round and round.

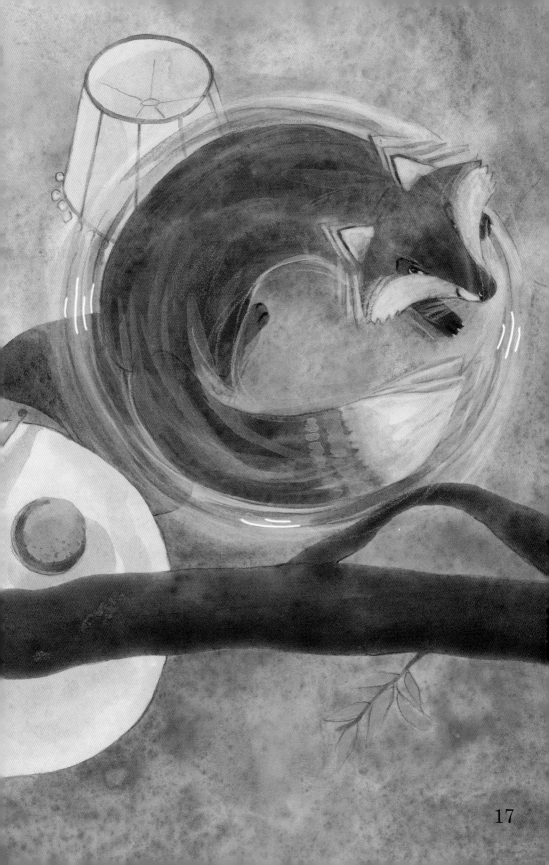

Red Hen's head went
round and round, too.
She fell down into
Sly Fox's big, black bag.

Sly Fox ran into the wood.
The big, black bag was
heavy and Sly Fox sat
down to rest. Then he
fell asleep.

Red Hen jumped out of the bag.

"You're the fox, you're the fox, you're really sly. But you won't catch me, however you try!" said Red Hen.

Red Hen put some
heavy stones in the bag.
Then she ran all the
way home.

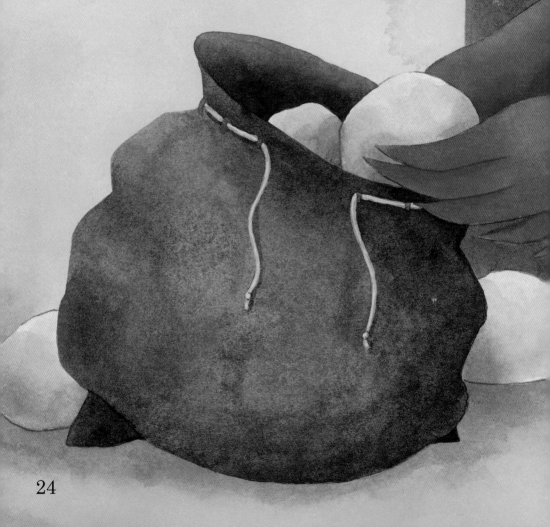

Sly Fox tipped the bag into the cooking pot.

"I'm the fox, I'm the fox, I'm really sly. I will eat you. Say goodbye!"

The stones fell SPLASH!
into the cooking pot.

"Oh no!" said Sly Fox.
"I did not catch Red Hen!"

How much do you remember about the story of Sly Fox and Red Hen? Answer these questions and find out!

- **Where does Red Hen live?**

- **Where does Sly Fox live?**

- **How does Sly Fox catch Red Hen?**

- **What does Red Hen put in the bag?**

Look at the pictures and match them to the story words.

Red Hen

Sly Fox

stones

bag

wood

Read it yourself with Ladybird

Tick the books you've read!

For beginner readers who can read short, simple sentences with help.

Level 2

 Beauty and the Beast ☐

 Chicken Licken ☐

 Little Red Riding Hood ☐

 Nature Trail ☐

 Sports Day ☐

 Pirate School ☐

 Rumpelstiltskin ☐

 Sleeping Beauty ☐

 The Gingerbread Man ☐

 Sly Fox and Red Hen ☐

 The Tale of Jemima Puddle-Duck ☐

 The Three Little Pigs ☐

 Why Lion Roarrrs! ☐

 The Big Race ☐

 Town Mouse and Country Mouse ☐

 Dom's Dragon ☐

For more confident readers who can read simple stories with help.

Level 3

 YOU won't like this present as much as I DO! ☐

 The Elves and the Shoemaker ☐

 Hansel and Gretel ☐

 Harry and the Bucketful of Dinosaurs ☐

 Jack and the Beanstalk ☐

 Furi on Music Island ☐

 Poppet Stows Away ☐

 Rapunzel ☐

 The Red Knight ☐

 Available on the App Store

The Read it yourself with Ladybird app is now available for iPad, iPhone and iPod touch

App also available on Android devices